HIS NIGHTLY OBSESSION

MEN OF THE SEA BOOK TWO

SADIE KING

LET'S BE BESTIES!

A few times a month I send out an email with new releases, special deals and sneak peeks of what I'm working on. If you want to get on the list I'd love to meet you!

You'll even get a free short and steamy romance when you join.

Sign up here:
www.authorsadieking.com/free

HIS NIGHTLY OBSESSION

MEN OF THE SEA

HIS NIGHTLY OBSESSION

I'm a simple fisherman with a dark secret...

Ever since I saw the curvy, troubled Mira, I knew she needed my protection.

I watch her at night, following her every move.

Her dreams become my dreams. Her burdens become my burdens to dispose of.

I'm a fisherman by day, her caretaker by night.

But she must never know what I've done to keep her safe, to protect what's mine...

His Nightly Obsession is a steamy instalove romance featuring an OTT obsessed man and the curvy woman he claims as his own.

PROLOGUE

*W*ater laps softy against the prow of the dinghy as my oars dip beneath the surface.

Clouds cover the moon, making the ocean a black moving mass. But I know my way around the bay. I know how to row silently, avoiding the rocks and staying out of the beams from car headlights on the road.

I move quietly through the water, out of the marina and away from the jetty, leaving the lights of the township far behind.

Outside the shelter of the bay, the sea is choppy, and my heavy cargo rocks side to side in the bottom of the dinghy.

Putting all my strength into it, I row.

I row until the lights of the mainland shrink to dots. I row until my shoulders ache. I row until the waves of the open ocean slosh over the side of the skiff, wetting my pants.

I row until we're over the place where the ocean floor drops off into the depths of the trench below.

Only then do I secure the oars and roll my aching shoulders.

The lights of Temptation Bay are tiny specks, barely visible.

Mira is behind one of those lights.

I try to make out which is her apartment above the cafe, which light she's behind, and I wonder what she's doing now. Her soft, curvy body is probably lying in bed, her silken hair spread out on the pillow as she breathes softly. Asleep.

How I long to be lying next to her rather than out here in the cold, tending to business. I imagine sliding into bed next to Mira's warm body. The feel of her curves molding to my frame. The taste of her lips on my tongue.

But if Mira knew what I was out here doing, she wouldn't want anything to do with me.

I'm just a simple fisherman. That's what everyone in town believes I am. And that must be what Mira believes too.

My cargo is heavy, wrapped in sacking and tied with thick rope.

Crouching in the dinghy, I heave my cargo to the edge and push it over the side. The splash as it hits the water is drowned out by the waves. The package tilts on its end before quietly sinking below the dark surface.

There are boulders tied within that will help it sink, tugging it all the way down to the bottom of the trench.

Over time, the water will wear away at the sacking, and the fish will nibble at what's inside until there's nothing left.

With my business completed for the night, I pick up the oars and row for home.

MIRA

The fat crackles and spits, sending hot flecks of breadcrumbs onto my apron. Grabbing the basket, I lift it onto the rack to drain. At the same time, I grab two plates and dump a handful of lettuce onto them.

In my haste, I accidentally knock my elbow against the edge of the fryer and pain flares up my arm, awakening the purple bruise hidden under my sleeve.

Gritting my teeth, I push the pain aside. It's the tail end of a busy lunch rush, and customers are waiting for their meals. There's no time to dwell on the bruises on my body. Besides, I've gotten used to working with the constant dull ache.

I get the fish out of the basket and onto the plate for table thirty-eight, who have been waiting far too long for their lunch.

"Two fish and chips."

"Thank you, dear."

The middle-aged couple, relaxed and windswept from their day at the coast, give me a warm smile, and I force my lips to turn up at the corners in return.

Only to see their smile disappear when they see the size of their fish portions. Before they can say anything, I turn away, hastily retreating to the kitchen.

Ever since Uncle went on a cost cutting mission, I've had to endure the complaints of customers.

The portions are smaller, you have to pay for ketchup and water, and anything expensive has disappeared from the menu.

I may own half of Something Fishy Café, but my uncle controls everything.

My throat's parched and there's a rumble in my belly, but the cafe's a mess from the last of the lunch rush, and if I take a break before it's clean, Uncle won't like it.

Grabbing a plate from the top of the stack, I scrape the leftovers off and slide it into the dishwasher.

The bell above the cafe jingles, and I try not to be annoyed that there's yet another customer. I need to get the dishes clean or I'll get in trouble with Uncle.

"I'll be with you in a minute," I call, trying to keep the irritation from my voice.

With the dishwasher full, I switch it on and come out to the counter, wiping the sweat from my forehead.

My hand stops on my head, and my breath catches in my throat.

Standing at the counter—all six-foot something with a grizzled beard, chiseled face lined from the wind, and the softest blue eyes I've ever come across—is Sean.

The tension drains out of my body, and I give my first genuine smile of the day. The smile I reserve for my fisherman, as I like to call him.

"What you got today?"

I sweep a strand of hair off my sticky forehead and try to tuck it behind my ear. I wish I wasn't always wearing a grease-stained apron whenever I see him. But my fisherman doesn't seem to mind.

His blue eyes regard me slowly, running over my too tight t-shirt and hip hugging skirt that Uncle insists I wear halfway up my leg, even though I hate the way it shows off my too thick thighs.

"Some people like a girl they can grab," is what Uncle said when I tried to let out the hem. His eyes on my legs narrowed, and he licked his lips in a way that made my blood go cold.

Ever since I was left in Uncle's care and made half owner of the cafe he and Dad ran together, his looks have been getting more and more predatory.

The way Sean looks at me is different.

His soft eyes take me in, a small frown forming at the sight of my exposed thighs. I tug at the hem self-consciously, and his gaze moves back to my face.

When his eyes meet mine, they're full of heat. It's a soft heat, a gentle heat simmering under the surface that I long to unleash. A heat that makes my body tremble and a strange sensation tug between my legs.

"I saved a dozen crabs for you."

He's talking about his catch. But the way he says it, low and deep, makes me hot around the neck.

"We're not serving crab anymore."

It's one of Uncle's new rules. Too expensive to buy, and he doesn't want to make the cafe too fancy, he says. It might price the locals out. Even though the locals love crab, and the tourists more so. But it's no use arguing with Uncle. I've got the bruises to prove it.

"Guess I've got some spare crab then."

Sean rubs his beard slowly, watching me in a way that makes my skin flush. His hands are callused, raw from the ocean and pulling ropes. I wonder what those rough hands would feel like on my soft, untouched body.

Heat spreads up my neck, and I look down, hoping he doesn't know what I'm thinking about him.

"Come by my boat after work, and I'll cook some up for you."

My heart stops for a minute as I process what he's just said. Sean, the silent fisherman I've been lusting after ever since I can remember, just asked me out.

I glance at his face to see if he's joking. I'm the chubby, sweaty girl who works in the local cafe, who he talks to briefly when he drops off his catch. Can he really be asking me out?

His face is sincere, his pale eyes regarding me curiously. For a moment, I imagine what it would be like to sit with him on the jetty, dipping fresh crab in mayonnaise and sipping a beer as we watch the sunset, talking and laughing as if life were good.

But life isn't good. I live with my controlling uncle who'd probably kill both of us if I did anything like go on a date with a man.

"I'm busy," I mumble, lowering my eyes.

Sean nods slowly, and I can't bear to look at him.

"Mira…" My name on his lips makes my chest constrict. His voice is soft and deep, like the rumbling ocean.

"I'll be here when you're ready to live."

The words confuse me. I'm living, aren't I? If you can call this existence living. But what more can I do with Uncle following my every move?

As if I've conjured him from hell, Uncle crashes in from the back kitchen door that leads to the apartment upstairs that we share.

My body tenses, and my arms go protectively around my chest.

Sean watches me, frowning.

"You need to go," I say quickly. "Leave the fish at the back door."

But he makes no move to leave.

"Please." My voice comes out desperate, but I know what Uncle will do if he thinks I'm flirting with a local.

Sean looks uncertain, but he must see the desperation on my face.

"If that's what you want, Mira."

He turns to leave as Uncle strides to the counter, a scowl on his face. He takes one look at Sean's retreating back and his eyes narrow.

"You whore," he hisses so low that only I can hear. His fingers grab the fleshy part of my arm, squeezing my skin in a painful pinch that makes my eyes water.

"Whoring with the locals, are you? I bet you're fucking every man in town."

It's whispered into my ear so the customers can't hear. The gold ring that he wears presses into my cheek, and I know it's going to leave a red mark.

My body's shaking, but I've learned to shut it out, to not react. I shut my eyes tight and count slowly as I wait for it to be over.

My uncle pushes me away in disgust, and I stagger backward.

"Clean this fucking kitchen, girl."

I scramble for the cloth. "Yes, Uncle."

"I take you in, feed you, house you, and this is how you treat me…" he mutters to himself, but I block it out, rhythmically running the cloth over the greasy surfaces.

I've heard it all before. How hard he has it. The promise he made to my father to look after me, to give me shelter and a job at the cafe, and how I've been nothing but trouble.

Dad couldn't have known how his brother would treat

me. Like his personal slave. Like his punching bag to push around.

I block out what Uncle's saying and go to the imaginary place in my mind. The place where I'm eating fresh crab with Sean while watching the sunset. A place that can only ever exist in my imagination.

2

SEAN

The golden light of sunset glances across the deck and hits the water of Temptation Bay. From out in the bay, the township looks peaceful, bathed in the orange glow of sunset.

My hands are sticky from breaking apart freshly cooked crab, and I take a swig of beer to wash it down. Fresh seafood, beer, and a sunset. The only thing missing is Mira.

Wiping my hands on a cloth, I pick up my binoculars and train them on her apartment above the cafe.

I can't say when I started watching Mira, when the doleful girl with the sad eyes and killer curves caught my attention.

I just know that for the last several weeks, I've taken my boat out of the marina and found a spot in the bay. It's the perfect spot to watch the sunset. Only I face the other way.

Through my binoculars, I watch Mira as she sweeps the cafe, pausing to look out to the ocean. I watch how she stacks the chairs, taking her time closing up so she doesn't have to go upstairs.

When she locks the cafe, I wait until she appears in the

little window above, where the apartment she shares with her uncle is.

I watch her go into the kitchen where, after a long day of making meals for customers, she cooks for her uncle, stopping often to gaze out at the sunset.

I follow her through the window to the next room. She sits alone. Her uncle eats in front of the TV. Mira eats at the table.

I watch the curve of her neck, the movement of her lips, the way she looks out of the window with her hands resting on her chin, dreaming.

Tonight is no different. I can almost hear her sigh.

It started as a pastime, watching Mira. But it's become an obsession.

I've learned all about Mira. How her father passed away when she was twelve. I've learned all about her uncle who was tasked with protecting her but instead bullies her.

My anger has been growing, building inside me.

Today when she lifted her arm, I saw the bruises. I'm sure she gets them from him, although I have no proof.

But her fear of him in the cafe makes me almost certain.

There's movement at the window. Mira stands up quickly, and another figure comes into view. Her uncle, his face screwed up and red.

He's yelling at her. She flinches as he raises his hand. The blow comes swiftly to her upper arm, and I feel it all the way in my bones.

My jaw clenches and my fist pounds the decking.

No one hurts Mira.

A red mist descends over my vision. I've watched her for too long. It's time to act.

Someone's hurting my woman, and they will pay.

3

MIRA

The sounds of cawing seagulls wake me the next morning. Light streams through my window, and I sit up quickly, instantly regretting it as pain shoots through my arm.

Wincing, I shuffle out of bed and into the bathroom.

If I've slept in past sunrise, then I'm late to open the cafe. I need to get the coffee machine warmed up and the first batch of pastries out and ready for the early risers.

Expecting a harsh rap from my uncle at any minute, I'm surprised when I haven't heard from him by the time I finish my shower and dress.

Maybe he's slept in too. Or he's already in the cafe, waiting to scold me when I turn up late.

With trepidation, I hurry down the stairs and into the cafe.

It's quiet and empty. No sign of Uncle.

There's no time to think about it too much. I turn the fryer on to heat and pull out the pastry trays.

It's a beautiful sunny morning as I open the doors and set the tables for a day of serving. The bay looks beautiful on a day like today, the water still and calm with sunlight skimming off the surface.

I stop for a moment to drink it in. This is what makes my life bearable. The fresh sea air, open water, and sunshine.

I stand for a moment, letting the sun warm my face, before I duck inside and get ready for the first customers.

Uncle doesn't come into the cafe that day. Though I barely notice because I'm used to running it on my own anyway.

He's not at home when I close up either.

He's probably gone to stay with one of his women up the coast. I make myself a sandwich for dinner and eat it in front of the TV. A rare treat.

I make sure I clean up after myself, though. I can't be sure when he'll be back, and if the place is a mess, I'll pay for it.

Uncle doesn't show up the next day or the day after that.

Slowly, my bruises start to fade, and the tension I carry around eases.

I slide the hem down on my dress and give out free ketchup to my customers.

When another few days go past and Uncle still doesn't show, I begin to dream, to imagine him never coming back. I dream about what I'd do with the cafe, what I'd do with my life and who I'd have in it.

That night, I push the door to Uncle's room open. It smells musty. The bed's unmade, and clothes are strewn across the floor. His watch is on the bedside table, which strikes me as odd. Wherever he went, why wouldn't he take it?

An uneasy feeling grows in my gut. What if something's happened to Uncle? What if he never comes back?

On the sixth day, I call the police.

. . .

A detective comes while I'm sweeping up the cafe for the day. He asks me questions, and I answer as best I can.

I don't tell him about the bruises, or the pinching, or the red imprint of Uncle's ring on my skin that's only just fading.

The detective searches Uncle's room and makes some phone calls. But my uncle can't be found.

The next day, I'm humming to myself as I wipe down the counter. I tried a new salad recipe on the menu today.

Uncle would never let me experiment with the food. But with him not around, I can do what I like. The customers seem to love having a vegetarian option on the menu, and I've sold out of the salad. I'll have to buy more ingredients next time.

The bell rings, and I look up to see Sean coming through the door. I greet him with a shy smile. His eyes run over my face and he nods approvingly.

"You're looking good, Mira."

His soft voice makes my skin tingle, and heat pools in my core.

Without Uncle, I feel bold, more confident. I lean on the counter and am pleased to see Sean's eyes glance down at my cleavage.

"You got any crabs today? I'm putting crab back on the menu."

His eyes slowly move back to my face, stopping at my lips.

"You wanna come eat one with me later? Sail out and watch the sunset?"

My gut clenches with a familiar fear. Then I remember that without Uncle around, I can do what I please.

"Yeah," I say. Sean's cool eyes light up in a smile. "I'd like that."

He runs his hands through his beard, and the sight of his callused hands sends a shiver of anticipation through me.

"I'll come back for you after you lock up."

I watch him leave the cafe, feeling the lightest I've felt since I was twelve years old and got the news that Daddy had been killed in a motorbike accident.

Living with Uncle didn't start bad, but the last few years have been like living in a prison. I don't know what happened to my last living relative, or even if he's still alive.

But I feel lighter, happier, free for as long as it lasts.

4

SEAN

I did a bad thing.

I did a bad thing for Mira, and I don't regret it.

It was easy to follow Mira's uncle as he left the apartment late at night. Whether he was hurrying to his car to meet a woman or to head to the casino up the coast, I'll never know. It was easy to strike him down, fueled by my anger of his treatment of Mira. It was easy to row out to the deep ocean trench and dispose of her burden.

The next day, I watched Mira carefully. She was lighter without her uncle around. Her back straighter, her smile freer.

I felt anxious, sure that she must know what I've done. I waited a week before approaching her, gave her time to adjust so that she's not suspicious. Mira must never know what I did to protect her. To be with her.

I don't regret a thing as I watch her close up the cafe, her golden hair catching in the sunlight. She rewards me with a smile, and it washes away any doubts about what I've done. I'd do it again just to see that smile.

She's lighter as she walks. The hunched, haunted look is

gone, and with her newfound confidence, Mira is even more beautiful than ever.

As we walk to the marina, I take Mira's hand. It slots into mine, soft and warm, as if it's always belonged there.

We pass Will working on his boat and I give my neighbor a friendly wave. He raises an eyebrow when he sees my hand linked with Mira's but Will knows better than to say anything.

We're both good at not saying anything.

Will and I may seem like ordinary men, living on their boats and enjoying the quiet life, but we both have our secrets.

A man has to earn a living somehow and it's not easy around here. Will doesn't question me when I row out late and night and I don't question him if I'm coming back from a midnight run and see him sneaking into the marina with heavy pockets. A man's business is his own.

She boards my boat, and I take her out into the bay, anchoring at my favorite spot.

This time we face the sunset. I don't need to watch her window anymore. I've got Mira right here, where she belongs.

She sips a beer as I cook the crab. We eat it slowly, sitting on a blanket on the deck, talking about everything and nothing.

"My uncle's missing," she tells me.

I look for any sign of distress, any regret that he's missing. But there's none. She tells me all about it, including the police who don't seem interested, which is a relief. He had gambling debts and a string of angry women up the coast. The police think he disappeared.

"So, you own the cafe now?"

She stops short and looks at me. "I didn't think of that."

"I mean, if he doesn't come back."

She's lost in thought, her brow creased. "I'm sure he'll come back."

"But what if he doesn't, Mira?" I ask gently.

"I hope he's not dead. He's the only family I've got."

The words make me pause. I did this thing for her. This bad thing. It didn't occur to me she might miss her uncle.

"You've got me now."

I brush her cheek with my thumb, and she turns her dark eyes on me.

"I don't want you living in that apartment alone. Come. Stay on the boat with me. Let me look after you."

My callused thumb grazes her soft cheek. Her skin is so young, so tender. I long to run my hands all over her, to feel her give way underneath me.

"I've watched you for a long time, Mira." My hand slides down her throat, and I feel her pulse quicken under my touch. "Your uncle's gone. He's not coming back. If you want me, I'm yours."

Her eyes flicker open. Her lips part. "I want you, Sean. I've always wanted you."

My mouth closes over hers and our tongues collide. She's sweet and salty, and I kiss her gently, kissing away the pain, trying to make up for all the years I wasn't there, all the times I didn't act sooner to protect her.

The setting sun casts a golden glow over her skin, and I run my hands down her body. Her breath quickens, letting me know she likes it.

I promised myself I'd go slow, that I wouldn't pressure her. But my blood races through my veins as I peel off her top and unhook her bra, letting her soft breasts fall into my hands.

I killed for this woman, and I'm aching to claim my prize.

There's a cool sea breeze as I lay her down on the deck of the boat. Her nipples harden, and I close my mouth over one.

She gasps as I suck and nibble. My hand caresses the other nipple, then moves down her body to slip under her skirt.

It's been a long time that I've imagined doing this to Mira, and I've had to literally kill to get her here.

But as I taste her salty nipple and cup her damp pussy in my palm—by God, it was worth it. I'd kill a hundred men just to feel her body pressed against mine and her hot breath on my neck.

5

MIRA

*S*ean's teeth nibble at my breasts, his hot breath causing the skin to burn wherever it touches.

His rough hands slide over my body, the calluses grazing my skin. I've wanted this for so long, wanted him for so long. Now that it's happening, my body's on fire.

He lays me down on the wooden decking of the boat, a blanket beneath us. A cool sea breeze trails over my body, contrasting with the heat of his breath and causing a rippling sensation to pass right through me.

Water laps gently against the boat as the sun tints the sky a blazing red. I turn my head in the other direction and see the lights of the bay flickering to life. I can see the faint outlines of people walking along the shore or sitting on the rocks to watch the sunset.

Can they see us out here? Can they see me lying half naked on the deck of the boat?

Sean sits back on his knees, his gaze raking over my body. "You're beautiful."

He frowns at the bruises on my arms. They're faded, just a purple tinge. His breathing changes, and I can tell he's angry.

"I'm sorry I didn't protect you from this."

He runs a hand through his hair. I don't understand why he's distressed. It's Uncle's doing, not his. There's nothing Sean could have done to stop it.

"It's not your fault."

"I was too late," he mutters, and I'm not sure what means. "I promise from now on, I'll always protect you. I'll do whatever it takes to keep you safe."

Then he lowers his head and kisses each bruise. His finger traces each one with a tenderness that makes my heart ache.

Then his lips move to my throat, my neck, and my mouth.

A hand slides up my thigh and he cups my mound, gripping me in his palm. I whimper under his touch, and his gaze meets mine.

As his thumb moves slowly over my damp panties, his gaze penetrates me, and I glimpse something in his look—something dark.

"You're free now, Mira. Free to do whatever and be whoever you want."

His thumb strums my hard center, and even through my panties, his touch sends zaps of pleasure through my body. My hips push upwards, wanting more of whatever he's got to give.

"I want this." I've never felt so free in my life. My body tingles with new sensations. "I want you, Sean."

Sean's hand hooks under my panties, and he pulls them off my legs. I gasp as the cool evening air hits my pussy. Then his hand is back, clasping my pussy and stroking my hard nub, making me cry out.

I turn to the shore, wondering if anyone can hear me.

There's pressure at my entrance as Sean slides a finger inside me. My hips arch, my breath rushing out of my chest. All thoughts of those on shore are gone. I don't care if anyone sees or hears us. I only care about the sensation coming from my center.

"You're tight, Mira."

Sean's eyes are dark and hooded in the setting sun, but I can see the desire in them. "Are you a virgin?"

I bite my lower lip and nod, not sure if that's a good thing or not.

"I'll take care of you, baby girl."

His thumb strokes me softly, his finger pressing slowly inside of me. My eyelids flutter shut as I enjoy the sensations.

Sean is gentle for someone so rough. I feel cared for with Sean. Something I haven't felt for a long time.

There's a new sensation on my thigh. Scratchy and warm. My eyes fly open. Sean's head is between my legs, his mouth planting soft kisses on my thigh.

"What are you doing?" I gasp, the sensation almost making me lose control. I've never done anything like this before. I've never even had anyone to talk to about sex. I'm not sure what he's doing is normal.

"Relax, baby girl. I'm going to make sure you get the loving you deserve."

As he speaks, vents of warm air trail across my skin, making my core turn to liquid. I sit up on my elbows, fascinated as his mouth closes over my pussy.

"Oh my god." My eyes roll back into my head, and I fall backward onto the blanket. The sensations roll over me as he kisses my sensitive core.

I'm powerless. I'm completely at Sean's mercy.

He licks and strokes and fucks me with his tongue, his fingers. I gasp and moan as a pressure builds inside me.

"Sean…" I groan. "Something's happening."

He grips my hips and licks me harder as his fingers pump in and out of my pussy. My hands grip the blanket as the pressure bursts inside of me.

My core explodes and I cry out, not caring if the sound carries across the bay. My whole body shatters into a million pieces of energy that zap through me like hot white liquid. My pussy pulses, throbbing against his tongue.

I'm fisting the blanket with my back arched, letting the orgasm race through me.

When the tremors stop, I open my eyes. Sean is kneeling over me. My pussy juices glisten in his beard and I sit up, kissing him and tasting myself on his lips.

The sun is almost set, but in the dim light, I see the desire in his eyes.

I fumble with his jeans and pull out his hard cock. I've had a taste, and now I want all of him.

He pushes me gently onto my back and lines himself up with my entrance. The tip of his cock grazes my swollen lips. Then he pushes inside. I buck my hips, crying out at the new sensation. There's a stab of pain, and then he's inside me, filling me up and making me whole.

"Mira…" His hands stroke my cheek and we rock together, moving in time to the ocean gently rocking the boat.

He takes it slow, giving me time to get used to the new feeling, the delicious feeling of him inside of me. He slides slowly in and out of me as his rough hands trail over my throat, my breasts, my belly.

His thrusts become quicker, more urgent. I wrap my legs around his back, tilting my hips upward.

As he moves inside me, I feel the pressure build, and I know I'm going to come again.

Gripping his shoulders, I cry out as the orgasm takes me. Sean slams hard into me and groans, his cum exploding inside me.

We rock together, clinging together. Just the two of us on the ocean as the sun sets behind us.

6

SEAN

'm awoken by the buzz of my phone. I fumble for it in the dark, not wanting to wake Mira.

It's a few nights later, and she's spread out in my bed, her hair splayed on the pillow as she breathes gently, deep in a peaceful sleep.

The last few days have been the happiest of my life. Waking up next to Mira, cupping her body in mine, and taking her when I need to.

It didn't take long to move her onto my boat. She packed up her few belongings from the apartment above the cafe, and I made space for her in my cabin—our cabin.

My phone screen illuminates her briefly in a blue light, her full lips slightly parted as she sleeps. I have a strong urge to ignore my phone, to kiss those lips, to pull her close and never let her go.

But when my phone buzzes in the middle of the night, it's wise not to ignore it.

I know what the text is going to say. There's only one person who texts me after midnight when there's no moon.

Dressing quietly, I creep out of the cabin, shutting the door behind me.

The tender is roped to the back of the boat, and it rocks gently when I step into it.

It's a dark night, with the moon waning and clouds covering the stars. It's nights like these when I get summoned to work.

I'm a simple fisherman, but there's another job I do. I never joined the Underground Crows MC, preferring a boat to a bike, but some of the boys I grew up with did.

I lend a hand when I can. I know this bay better than anyone, where the hidden rocks are, what the winds mean for the tides. I can navigate my way around in the dark. And I know where the deepest parts of the ocean are. How far you need to go out to drop something overboard that will never be found.

Mira thinks I'm just a fisherman, but I'm more than that. I'm the fucking ferryman, rowing bad men to the shores of Hades.

Taking the oars in my hands, I begin to row.

7

MIRA

Four weeks later…

I'm humming to myself as I wipe down the galley of the boat, bringing a nice sheen back to the glossy wood.

The last four weeks have been the happiest of my life. Uncle hasn't made an appearance, and I'm beginning to believe he's gone for good.

It was easy to find a woman to help in the cafe, and she rents the apartment upstairs.

I boxed Uncle's things up and stored them in the attic, then got the locks changed. If he comes back, he'll find things different around here.

I've made changes to the menu, reintroducing fresh crab and other seafood dishes. We're busier than ever, so even with the new help, I'm there most days.

This afternoon is one of my rare days off, and I'm humming to myself as I clean the boat.

Sean's out with the other fishermen from town on a

shared boat they own together, leaving me alone in our new home.

It didn't take long to get used to living on the water, the smooth motion of the waves swaying me to sleep each night.

Sean has been gentle with me and attentive, accepting me into his life without question. It's like we were always meant to be, like we always will be.

Some nights I wake and his side of the bed is empty and cold. I know he goes wandering in the night. I looked for him once, but he wasn't on the boat and the dinghy was gone.

In the morning, he said nothing. So I said nothing.

I don't know where Sean goes at night, and I'm too scared to ask. My life now is better than anything I could have imagined. I don't want to ruin that. So, I say nothing.

I feel a thrill deep in my belly every time I think about Sean. Ever since he's come into my life, I feel free, lighter, like I have permission to take up space in the world. And the space I want to take is right next to Sean.

My fingers run over the wood paneling of the boat and, satisfied that it's clean, I head out onto deck to enjoy the sunshine.

The tender bumps against the stern of the boat, catching my attention.

There's a pile of old rags and rope in the bottom, and it looks like it could do with a good scrubbing. Treading carefully, I step into the dinghy and scoop up the bundle of rags.

Something slippery clings to my fingers, and I pull them away to see what I've poked my hand into.

My brow furrows. It looks like blood.

As I unwrap the rags, there's a rotten smell about them. The rags are stained dark, covered in blood. Fish blood, I tell myself. But an uneasy feeling starts in my stomach.

There's a thick coil of rope that the rags were stuffed into, and I stuff them back in it, breathing hard. Whatever Sean is doing with those, I don't want to know.

As I put the rags back, something falls out of them, clanging as it hits the bottom of the boat and rolls away under the seat.

Crouching down, I run my hand under the seat in search of the object.

My fingers close around something small and cool, and I pull out, turning it over in my hand.

My breath catches in my throat. The uneasiness in my gut multiplies.

It's a ring, but not just any ring. I'd recognize the thick gold crest ring anywhere. I should. It's been imprinted on my skin enough times. It's Uncle's ring.

8

SEAN

know something's wrong as soon as I see the boat.
Every day since I made her mine, Mira's waited
for me on the deck of the boat with a shy smile on her face.

Today, she's not there. A cold feeling starts in my gut as I clamber aboard.

"Mira?"

I find her in the galley. She's sitting with her knees tucked under her, her arms wrapped around her body.

"Everything okay?"

She holds out her hand, and there's something in her palm. I peer at the ring, waiting for it to mean something.

"It's my uncle's," she says accusingly. "I found it in the tender."

Ah shit. My blood goes cold. It must have fallen off of him when I had his body on the boat, pulled off his finger in my haste to shove him overboard.

My mind races to think of something to say. But there's no explanation I can give Mira.

She's staring at me, her expression hard as she waits for

an answer. I could lie to her. I could tell her I don't know why it's there or where it came from.

But this is the woman I want to spend my life with. She deserves the truth.

I pull at my beard, buying some time, not sure how to tell her.

"You did something, didn't you?"

It comes out as a whisper. Her expression is hurt, uncertain.

"He was a bad man, Mira. He hurt you. I couldn't stand by and watch that happen."

Her brow furrows in confusion. "So you…" She swallows, not able to say the words. "Killed him?"

I meet her gaze and nod slowly.

She lets out a gasp and looks away.

"I did it for you, Mira."

"I didn't ask you to." There're tears on her cheeks, and she swipes at them with the back of her hand.

My arm goes around her, wanting to comfort her, but she pushes me away. It's like a stab to the heart.

"I did it to protect you, Mira. And I'd do it again. I'd kill a hundred men if I had to."

She won't look at me. I take her chin in my hand. She snaps her head away.

"How about me? Would you hurt me?"

It's like a slap to the face. How could she even think I'd do anything to hurt her? "Of course not."

The hurt expression doesn't leave her face, and it's breaking my heart to see her like this.

"Where do you go, Sean? At night. When I wake up and you're not there. Where do you go?"

I sit back on my haunches.

She's looking at me fiercely, and if I have any chance of

holding onto her, I need to tell her the truth. It's time to come clean.

"I help the Crows out sometimes."

"The Underground Crows?" She raises her eyebrows. The MC gang doesn't have a great reputation around here, especially with someone as innocent as Mira.

"I grew up with some of the guys."

"And what exactly do you do for them, Sean?"

I rub my beard slowly.

It's painful the way she's looking at me, like she's disgusted with me, like she doesn't know me. And I hate how I look through her eyes: a rough seaman who aids outlaws for some extra cash. But that's not it. I know the bodies I drop into the ocean are bad men. They don't deserve to be on this earth making other people's lives miserable. I'm just not sure Mira sees it that way.

"I dispose of things for the Crows. I drop things that they don't want in the ocean."

I pick my words carefully, but she gets my meaning. Her face crinkles in disgust. "Is that what you did with Uncle? Is he in the ocean?"

I nod slowly. "He won't bother you anymore."

I put a hand on her thigh. She pushes it away. It cuts me up inside.

The woman I've been so close to the last few weeks. Sharing a bed with her. Sharing each other. Now she's looking at me like she doesn't know me at all.

"I need to leave." She stands up and I stand with her, my heart breaking.

"I'd do it again, Mira. I'd kill a hundred men to make you happy."

"Goodbye, Sean."

She stuffs some clothes into a bag, and I watch her leave. I don't try to stop her. I'll never forcibly lay a finger on that woman.

I don't regret what I did for Mira. Even if I can't have her, at least she's free.

But goddamn. Watching her walk down the jetty and away from me is the hardest thing I've ever had to do in my life.

9

SEAN

Two weeks later…

A seagull caws at me as I shuffle down the jetty. My bones are sore from a day out on the ocean, and all I want to do is get to my empty boat and drown my sorrows. It doesn't hold any joy for me anymore, my boat. Not since Mira walked out of my life.

I did what I had to do to protect her, and I don't regret it, but I sure as hell wish I could have kept hold of her.

Life is empty without Mira. Without her smile, without her touch. I don't even watch her through my binoculars anymore. She needs her space. I'll give it to her.

I get to my boat, and my heart stops beating for a moment. Sitting on the bow, her legs stretched out in front of her, is Mira.

I'm too stunned to speak. She looks good with her hair falling over her shoulder and her sweater pulled tight over her breasts.

"Mira."

She regards me with a cool look. The innocence has gone

from her face, and I regret that. But it's replaced with a more worldly expression, like she's grown up.

"I miss you, Sean."

The words are everything I've been wanting to hear. In one stride, I'm next to her, crouching by her side and wrapping my arms around her.

"I miss you too, sweetheart."

Her arms wrap around my neck, and she fixes her eyes on mine.

"I've thought about what you did."

I hold my breath. I hope she's here to forgive me, but I can't be sure. "It's the craziest, nicest thing anyone's ever done for me."

I let out my breath.

"I hated my uncle, really hated him. He hurt me, and it was only a matter of time before he did something worse."

"I'm telling you, Mira. Anyone hurts you, I'll do the same to them."

And I fucking mean it. I may be a simple fisherman, but where Mira's involved, I'll turn into a monster a hundred times over.

"I love you, Mira. I love you with everything that I am."

She wraps her arms around me. "I love you too."

I scoop her up and carry her down to the cabin. When I lay her on the bed, she sits up on her knees, her hand running over my chest.

"You're mine," I whisper into her neck. "Mine to protect. Mine to look after."

Her body presses against mine, and I ease her onto the bed, peeling her clothes off one by one until she's naked in front of me.

My hands run over her body, making her writhe with need. I take my time licking and sucking and tasting all of her.

She's mine to take care of, and I'll take care of her all right. It's not until she's crying my name in pleasure that I ease myself inside her dripping pussy, taking my pleasure in hers.

We rock together, gentle and calm, until we come together, the slow build of the orgasm making it more intense.

Once we've finished shuddering, we flop exhausted onto the bed.

Mira snuggles into me, and I wrap my arms around her. Now she knows what I am, that underneath the gentle fisherman, there are dark waters.

She knows what I am, and she's still here.

I'm the quiet fisherman no one notices. But you come for my woman, and I'm a fucking monster.

1 0

EPILOGUE

MIRA

Five years later…

"*S*hoo, shooo."

The seagulls scatter as Wade runs through them on his unsteady legs, sending them cawing angrily into the air.

He runs back to me, grinning. "I scared them, Mommy."

"Well done, sweetheart."

His sister stirs in the sling resting across my front, and it won't be long before she's crying for her milk.

We walk the short distance to the stone cottage set a few streets back from the waterfront. It's an old fisherman's cottage that's been restored and added to.

It used to belong to three siblings, until the scandal with the sisters. The town call it a scandal, I call it true love. I used to be friends with the wild Layla and it was no surprise when she ran off like she did. But her studious sister Coraline running off with an Underground Crow, well that was more surprising. But love has a funny way of taking you by surprise, I should know.

I give Mandy her milk and set her down on the play rug with her brother while I prep the food for dinner.

My mind goes to the cafe, thinking about what to put on the autumn menu. Once I had the children, I hired a cafe manager, but I still plan the menus and stop by most days to help out.

The Something Fishy Café has become a popular place with the locals and a destination stop for tourists travelling down the coast.

There was an opportunity to enter the running for a prestigious award, but I turned it down. We don't like drawing attention to ourselves in Temptation Bay. It's better if we're overlooked.

People may stop by for a few hours to visit the beach and have a seafood lunch, but then they keep on going down the coast. All they'll see here is a quiet seaside town.

It's better that way.

I make a hearty seafood chowder with freshly baked bread for dinner. Sean will be hungry when he comes in off the boat.

It's a few hours later when Sean comes in the door, windswept and salty from the ocean. His cool eyes light up when he sees me playing with the children.

I stand and kiss him as his hands slide around my waist. He pulls me to him, my burly fisherman with the rough hands.

His kiss is gentle, as he always is with me. But I know the passion that rages underneath. I know what my gentle giant is capable of.

Sometimes I think of my uncle, and I wonder at our dark secret, if we did the right thing. But then I remember the bruises, the unwanted looks, the bullying, and the violence.

My husband did what he had to do to protect me, and I'll be forever grateful for that.

He's more than just a simple fisherman. He's my life, my salvation, and my protector.

These days, we're just like any other young family.

But don't look too closely. Or you might see my husband leave the house in the dead of night. You might see him take the dinghy out on a moonless night to dispose of the dredges of the underworld.

You'd never know as you watch him hurl his son into the air, making him howl with laughter. My gentle giant. The fisherman. My protector.

THE BIKER'S REVENGE

She's my enemy's daughter and my new obsession.

After three years inside, there's only one thing I want: revenge.

But when a retaliation goes wrong, I find myself with a fire cat captive—Scarlett, my enemy's daughter.

She's half my age and dripping with innocence. Scarlett becomes my revenge, and it's never been sweeter. But when her father comes for her, there's no way I'm giving her up.

The Biker's Revenge is a forbidden love, age-gap romance that starts with a kidnapping and ends with a happily ever after. Featuring an OTT obsessed hero and the curvy girl he claims as his own.

mybook.to/UCBikersRevenge

GET YOUR FREE BOOK

Sign up to the Sadie King mailing list for a FREE book!

You'll be the first to hear about new releases, exclusive offers, bonus content and all my news. You can even email me back. I love chatting with my readers!

To claim your free book visit:
www.authorsadieking.com/free

SERIES BY SADIE KING

Sunset Coast

The Underground Crows MC

Sunset Security

Men of the Sea

Filthy Rich Love

Love and Obsession

Wild Heart Mountain

Military Heroes

Mountain Heroes

Wild Riders MC

Maple Springs

Men of Maple Mountain

All the Single Dads

Candy's Café

Small Town Sisters

Kings County

Kings of Fire

King's Cops

For a full reading list check out the Sadie King website

www.authorsadieking.com

ABOUT THE AUTHOR

Sadie King is a USA Today Best Selling Author of short instalove romance.

She lives in New Zealand with her ex-military husband and raucous young son.

When she's not writing she loves catching waves with her son, runs along the beach, and good wine, preferably drunk with a book in hand.

Keep in touch when you sign up for her newsletter. You'll even snag yourself a free short romance!

Visit: www.authorsadieking.com/free

www.authorsadieking.com